RAINBOW magic

PET FAIRIES

KATIE
THE KITTEN FAIRY

By Daisy Meadows
Illustrated by Georgie Ripper

Silver Dolphin

Silver Dolphin Books
An imprint of Printers Row Publishing Group
A division of Readerlink Distribution Services, LLC
9717 Pacific Heights Blvd, San Diego, CA 92121
www.silverdolphinbooks.com

Printers Row Publishing Group is a division of
Readerlink Distribution Services, LLC.
Silver Dolphin Books is a registered trademark of
Readerlink Distribution Services, LLC.

All notations of errors or omissions should be addressed to Silver Dolphin
Books, Editorial Department, at the above address. All other correspondence
(author inquiries, permissions) concerning the content of this book should be
addressed to:
Hachette Children's Group
Carmelite House
50 Victoria Embankment
London
EC4Y 0DZ

ISBN: 978-1-6672-0668-4
Manufactured, printed, and assembled in Guangzhou, China.
First printing, January 2024. GD/01/24
28 27 26 25 24 1 2 3 4 5

KATIE
THE KITTEN FAIRY

Fairies with their pets I see
and yet no pet has chosen me!
So I will get some of my own
to share my perfect frosty home.

This spell I cast, its aim is clear:
To bring the magic pets straight here.
The Pet Fairies soon will see
their seven pets living with me!

Table of Contents

A VERY UNUSUAL KITTEN

"Catch!"

Kirsty Tate tossed a baseball into the air. She watched as her friend Rachel Walker ran across the grass to catch it. It was the first day of spring break and Rachel had come to stay with Kirsty's family for a whole week. The two girls were in the

park while Kirsty's parents were at the grocery store. The sun was shining brightly, and there wasn't a cloud in the sky. It felt like perfect spring weather.

Rachel held up the ball triumphantly. "Your turn," she called. "Ready?"

Before Kirsty could reply, loud barking rang through the air. Both girls spun around to see a large black dog bounding past them.

Rachel jumped back as the dog raced by. "Is that a squirrel it's chasing?" she asked, watching the dog run off.

Kirsty shielded her eyes from the sun to take a better look. "No, it's a kitten!" she exclaimed. Her eyes widened at the sight of a tiny, gray kitten scrambling across the grass. "What's a kitten doing in the park?"

"I don't know—but that dog's about to catch it," Rachel said in alarm. "Come on!"

The two girls started to run after the animals. But they hadn't gotten very far before a sudden flash of bright light flickered through the air. A cloud of amber-colored sparkles swirled around the kitten. Seconds later, the kitten vanished—and an enormous striped tiger appeared in its place! The tiger turned toward the dog and roared.

Right away, the dog stopped short and put its ears back. Then, with a frightened whimper, it turned and bolted away as quickly as it could.

Kirsty and Rachel watched in disbelief as the tiger turned back into a kitten with another flash of bright sparkles.

The kitten shook itself off, licked one paw, and padded off happily through the grass.

Rachel rubbed
her eyes. "Did
you just see that?"
she asked, her
eyes still fixed on
the kitten.

Kirsty nodded.
"That looked like
fairy magic!" she
exclaimed.

Rachel grinned.
"That's exactly
what I thought,"
she replied. Whenever she and Kirsty
were together, they always had the best
magical adventures. This looked like it
might be the start of another one!

Then Rachel paused thoughtfully. "But
. . . we haven't seen any fairies here!"

Kirsty frowned. "That is strange, isn't it?" she said. "Let's follow the kitten. Maybe it will lead us to a fairy!"

The two girls hurried after the small kitten. It didn't seem to be in any real rush as it wandered along, stopping to pounce on a daisy or bat at a blade of grass.

"Where do you think its going?"
Rachel whispered. "It seems like it's
heading right for that fence."

They both watched as the kitten walked
cheerfully toward a wooden fence at
the edge of the grass. The fence was too
high for the kitten to climb over, but it
showed no sign of changing direction.

"How is the kitten going to—" Kirsty
started. Then she broke
off in surprise.

With another swirl of
sparkles, the kitten had
suddenly shrunk!
Now it was the size
of a mouse, small
enough to squeeze
through a tiny hole at
the bottom of the fence.

Kirsty's eyes widened as she watched its little gray tail disappear through the hole.

"Wow!" Rachel gasped, staring after the kitten. "Quick—there's a gate in the fence over that way. We can't lose track of that kitten!"

Both girls rushed through the gate, and saw that the kitten was now full-size again. The only sign that it had ever been any different was a faint trail of magical sparkles glimmering behind it.

Just then, the kitten twitched its whiskers and bounded toward a food cart. As the girls got closer, they saw it run up to a man who was standing by the vendor.

"Fish sticks and fries, please," the girls heard him say.

The kitten meowed loudly. It wound itself between the man's legs as the vendor handed him a plateful of food.

The man chuckled. "Sorry, kitty," he said, sitting down on a nearby bench. "This is my lunch, not yours."

As the man began to eat, Kirsty elbowed Rachel and nodded toward the kitten. Its eyes were glowing a bright green.

A small cloud of amber-colored sparkles glittered in the air as the kitten looked up hopefully at the man's food.

A second later, a fish stick tumbled off the man's plate and landed at the kitten's feet!

With a happy meow, the kitten
pounced on the
fish stick and
began to eat it.

The man
laughed. "It's
your lucky day,
kitty," he said.
"How did I
knock that off the plate?"

Rachel and Kirsty grinned at each
other. They knew that the sneaky kitten
had used magic to make the fish stick
fall to the ground.

"That was definitely fairy magic!"
Kirsty exclaimed. She watched as the
kitten gobbled up the fish stick, cleaned
its whiskers, and trotted off down a
tree-lined path.

"Yes," Rachel agreed. "Something strange is going on! Let's see where the kitten goes now." The girls set off after the kitten again.

They hadn't gotten far when they heard a scuffling sound along the side of the path. Suddenly, six green goblins jumped out from behind a tree! They were clutching butterfly nets.

"There it is!" shouted one of the goblins, pointing at the kitten. "Get it!"

SURPRISE ATTACK!

"Goblins!" Kirsty cried in surprise.
"Oh, no!"

At the sight of the goblins, the
kitten's fur stood up like a prickly brush.
It hissed at the goblins, then turned and
ran away from them, toward the girls.
With nowhere else to go, it leaped right
up into Rachel's arms!

"Oh!" Rachel gasped, surprised to find the little bundle of fur in her arms. She held the kitten protectively as the goblins approached.

"Give us that kitten!" one of the them ordered. "It belongs to Jack Frost, and we've been sent to bring it home," he added.

Kirsty and Rachel hesitated. They'd
met Jack Frost's goblins many times
before, and knew what sneaky creatures
they could be. Could they really trust
the goblins to be
telling the truth?

The kitten gave
a soft meow, and
both girls looked
down at it. Its eyes
were shining bright
green again. Sparkles
streamed out of its mouth and swirled
around in the air! The kitten meowed
again, but this time the girls could hear
words in its meows.

"Don't believe those terrible goblins,"
the kitten declared. "I belong to Katie
the Kitten Fairy, but I'm lost!"

Kirsty's fingers quickly closed over the locket around her neck. She and Rachel had been given matching gold lockets full of fairy dust by the Fairy King and Queen. The fairy dust would take them straight to Fairyland if they ever needed help. Now seemed like a very good time to use the lockets!

"We don't believe you," Rachel told the goblins. "And you're not getting this kitten!" Just then, Kirsty threw golden fairy dust all over herself, Rachel, and the kitten.

With angry cries, two of the goblins dropped their butterfly nets and dove toward the girls. They stretched their gnarled green hands out to grab the kitten.

Rachel yelped and tried to dodge out of the way, but luckily, the fairy dust was already working its magic. The girls were swept up into the sky. Below them, the goblins pounced on empty air and fell onto the grass.

Rachel and Kirsty laughed in relief as they felt the fairy dust whisking them through the air. After a moment, they couldn't see the park below, just a blur of bright, sparkling colors all around them. Rachel held the kitten close, in case it was frightened. It seemed used to fairy magic, though, and snuggled up happily in Rachel's arms. Its little ears blew back in the warm, sparkly breeze.

Moments later, the girls floated softly down to the ground. As the magical breeze died away, they both smiled to see that they were back in Fairyland.

"We're fairies!" Rachel exclaimed happily, fluttering her delicate wings.

"And there's the fairy palace, and the king and queen!" Kirsty cheered, waving as King Oberon and Queen Titania approached. Then she frowned.

"They don't look very happy, though."

Rachel watched as the king and queen came closer, followed by a crowd of anxious-looking fairies. Her excitement at being back in Fairyland disappeared as she saw how unhappy they all looked. Something was clearly troubling them. What was wrong?

MISSING PETS!

"Hello, Your Majesties," Rachel said politely, giving the king and queen a curtsy with the kitten still in her arms. "Is everything all right?"

A fairy in a pale yellow dress with long, dark hair suddenly caught sight of the kitten. A happy smile lit up her face.

"You've brought Shimmer back!" she cried. "Oh, thank you, thank you!"

The kitten jumped out of Rachel's arms and scampered over to the pretty fairy. The fairy scooped her up, burying her face in Shimmer's soft, silky fur.

"Thank you so much," she said, putting Shimmer down and turning to hug Kirsty and Rachel.

"I'm Katie the Kitten Fairy, and I can't tell you how glad I am to see Shimmer back in Fairyland!"

"You're welcome," Rachel said, smiling.

The king and queen stepped forward.

"How nice to see you again, girls," the king said warmly. "These are our Pet Fairies. You've already met Katie. This is Bella the Bunny Fairy, Georgia the Guinea Pig Fairy, Lauren the Puppy Fairy, Harriet the Hamster Fairy, Molly the Goldfish Fairy, and Penny the Pony Fairy."

Each fairy stepped forward when her name was called and curtsied to the girls with a little smile. Kirsty couldn't help noticing that their smiles looked a bit sad.

"So where are all the other pets?" she asked curiously.

The fairies all sighed. "Jack Frost stole them," Queen Titania told the girls sadly. "He took them to his ice castle, then sent out a ransom note. It said that if the Pet Fairies couldn't find him a pet of his own, he would keep all their magic pets for himself."

"Oh, no!" Kirsty cried out. "He can't do that!"

"He already has," the king responded. "And without their magic pets, the Pet Fairies can't look after all the pets in your world."

"The Pet Fairies are responsible for helping pets that are lost or homeless," the queen explained. "But they can't do that if their own magic pets are missing."

"Can't we give Jack Frost another pet, so that he'll let the magic pets go?" Rachel suggested.

The queen shook her head. "I'm afraid it's not that simple." She sighed. "In Fairyland, pets *choose* their owners. And no pet has ever chosen Jack Frost."

"I'm not surprised!" Kirsty blurted out. Jack Frost was always causing trouble in Fairyland. No wonder none of the magic pets wanted to live with him!

The king was gazing at Shimmer with a thoughtful expression on his face. "Kirsty, Rachel, where did you find Shimmer?" he asked. "We thought all the magic pets were locked in Jack Frost's ice castle."

"She was wandering around in the local park," Kirsty replied. "She looked lost!"

The kitten gave a sudden loud meow, as if she was joining in the conversation. Katie listened hard, then nodded. "Shimmer says that all the magic pets were all being kept in Jack Frost's castle," she said. "But they managed to escape, and now they're all roaming around in the human world."

The Pet Fairies looked very happy to hear this, but Shimmer was still meowing.

Katie listened again, then bit her lip. "Jack Frost has sent out a group of goblins to catch them and take them back to the ice castle," she announced anxiously. "Oh, our poor little pets!"

The other Pet Fairies gasped, and the king and queen looked worried, too.

"We have to find the pets before the goblins do!" the queen said, sounding determined.

Kirsty and Rachel looked at each other. Then, at the same time, they said, "We'll help!"

GIRLS ON GUARD

All the fairies cheered when the girls agreed to help.

"Thank you!" King Oberon said, smiling. "It's very kind of you to help us once again."

"The magic pets may be hard to find," Queen Titania warned them. "In Fairyland, they are tiny, fairy-size pets, but in the human world, they

can be any size they wish. They can also
work some fairy magic of their own, so
you will have to look very carefully."

Shimmer meowed suddenly and Katie
bent her head to listen. Her face turned
serious. "Shimmer said that a kitten in the
human world needs
our help," she told
the others. "It has
no home. Shimmer
and I need to find
one for it!"
Katie turned to the
king and queen.
"Can we go rescue
the kitten?"

The king and queen both hesitated.
"We'd love you to help . . ." the queen
began slowly.

"But we don't want the goblins to catch Shimmer," the king finished.

"Maybe we could go with Katie and Shimmer," Kirsty suggested. "We could protect them from the goblins!"

The king and queen looked at each other.

Then Queen Titania nodded. "That would be all right," she said. "That's very nice of you girls. But you must all be careful. You know how tricky and mean the goblins can be."

"We'll be careful," Katie said, her face lighting up. "Let's go!" She waved her wand, and a trail of amber-colored fairy dust trailed from it.

The dust trickled down around Kirsty and Rachel, and suddenly, Fairyland blurred before their eyes. A magical wind swept them up, and they flew through the air with Katie and Shimmer.

In a rush of color and light, the girls found themselves back in their own world. They were human-size once again!

"We're back in the park," Rachel said, looking around. "Watch out for goblins, everyone!"

Katie was still holding tiny Shimmer. She flew to hide on Kirsty's shoulder while the girls looked around for goblins.

The magic kitten jumped down from Katie's arms and curled up on Kirsty's shoulder. Kirsty could feel his little tail twitching back and forth.

"That tickles!" Kirsty giggled as Shimmer batted playfully at her hair.

"The coast is clear," Rachel said, after the girls scanned the park. "Let's start looking for a homeless kitten."

"We'll have to search carefully," Katie advised. "If it's scared, it could have hidden somewhere."

The four of them set off, keeping their ears open for meows. Katie flew between the girls at shoulder height, while Shimmer padded along beside her in midair.

How fascinating to watch him, Kirsty thought.

Even though the tiny kitten was hovering magically in the air, he moved as if he were on the ground. Sometimes he padded along, occasionally he pounced, and every so often he stopped to stalk a floating dandelion seed, or to chase his own fluffy tail. He seemed particularly interested in the elastic holding Rachel's ponytail, which had a couple of pink stars dangling from it. A few times, he leaped up to catch the stars between his tiny paws.

"Come on, Shimmer, we've got work to do," Katie reminded him.

She fluttered over to scoop him out of Rachel's hair. "Where could that lost kitten be?"

Suddenly, Shimmer pricked up his ears and stopped. His little pink nose turned up and his whiskers twitched as he sniffed the air. Then he took a flying leap down to the ground in a bright burst of sparkles, and he grew to the size of a normal kitten! Shimmer raced off ahead of the girls toward the playground.

"I think he found the kitten!" Katie smiled, flying behind her pet. "Come on, girls!"

Rachel and Kirsty ran after Shimmer as he bolted through the grass. Just before he reached the playground, he swerved toward a tall elm tree and sat at the bottom, looking up at it.

Kirsty, Rachel, and Katie gazed up to see what Shimmer had found. On one of the highest branches, huddled against the trunk and looking down at them with big golden eyes, sat a tiny tabby kitten.

SHIMMER'S PLAN

"Poor little thing!" Kirsty exclaimed.
"It's only a baby!"

Just then, a breeze blew through the
tree, and the tabby kitten pounced
on a leaf that was flapping nearby. It
almost lost its balance and tumbled out
of the tree!

"Careful, kitty," Katie called up. The kitten sat down and started washing its paws.

Shimmer ran a little way up the tree toward the tabby kitten and started meowing. The kitten meowed back eagerly.

"Oh, the poor kitten climbed the tree to get out of the wind last night and now it's stuck!" Katie translated Shimmer and the other kitten's meows.

"It's too scared to climb back down." "Should I climb up and get it?" Rachel offered. Before Katie could reply, Shimmer started meowing again. The fairy listened, then looked over at the nearby playground. "Good idea, Shimmer," she said, smiling. Then she turned back to the girls. "Thanks for the offer, Rachel, but Shimmer has someone else in mind for the job," she explained with a grin.

She pointed her wand in the direction of the playground. "See that boy in a red shirt at the top of the jungle gym?" she asked.

"The one with black hair?" Kirsty said, squinting.

Katie nodded. "That's the one," she

replied. "Would you go and ask him if he can help you get the kitten down from the tree?"

"OK," Kirsty agreed, confused.

"Trust me," Katie said. "It's very important that it is that boy who rescues this kitten." She winked at the girls. Shimmer meowed loudly, as if he was agreeing with Katie.

"All right," Rachel laughed. "Come on, Kirsty!"

Shimmer shrank back down to fairy pet size. He and Katie hid in the tree while Rachel and Kirsty ran over to the playground. The dark-haired boy had just jumped off the jungle gym when the girls arrived.

"Hello," Kirsty said, giving him a friendly smile. "I'm Kirsty, and this is Rachel. Could you help us rescue a kitten? It's stuck in a tree."

"We saw how good you are at climbing," Rachel explained. "We were wondering if you could climb up the tree and get it down?"

"Sure," the boy replied eagerly. "My name is James, and I love cats. Where's the kitten?"

The girls pointed out the elm tree. James yelled over to tell his dad to let him know where he was going. Then he followed Kirsty and Rachel to the tree.

James looked up at the kitten. "Don't worry, little kitten! I'll have you down in two minutes," he called and began to climb.

Kirsty and Rachel watched as he clambered higher and higher. Just as he was about to reach the branch that the tabby kitten was perched on, the kitten jumped down onto James's shoulder and butted its head gently against the boy's cheek.

Kirsty blinked. It looked like a haze of amber-colored sparkles surrounded James and the kitten. She glanced at Rachel and they grinned knowingly—more Pet Fairy magic!

James carefully carried the tabby kitten all the way back down to the ground. "It's so tiny," he marveled, stroking the kitten gently. "I wonder where it lives."

"It doesn't have a collar or a nametag," Kirsty said. "It looks like a stray."

"Here comes my dad," James said, as a tall, dark-haired man strolled

over. "Dad, look! We found a lost kitten!" His eyes brightened suddenly. "Hey, Dad—can we keep it?"

James's dad smiled. "Your mom and I have been talking about getting you a pet," he said. "But we can't just take this one without checking to make sure it doesn't belong to someone else." He looked around to see if the kitten's owner was somewhere in the park.

"We've been here for awhile," Kirsty said politely. "Nobody seems to be looking for the kitten."

"Please?" James asked quickly, as soon as his dad hesitated. "We can take it home with us, and call the animal shelter from our house." He stroked it again. "Oh, it's purring, Dad. It likes me!"

James's dad ruffled his son's hair. "OK then," he said. "If nobody's reported the kitten missing, then I think you can keep it."

"Hooray!" cheered James, beaming from ear to ear. He tickled the tabby kitten under its chin, and the kitten purred even louder. "Do you think Dusty would be a good name?" James wondered aloud.

Rachel nudged Kirsty. She had spotted a few more flecks of fairy dust twinkling in the air around James and the kitten! "Oh, Dusty would be a wonderful name," she said, trying not to giggle.

"Well, then, Dusty," James's dad said, petting the kitten, "we'd better take you home!"

GRASPING GOBLINS

The girls watched as James and his dad walked away happily with their new kitten.

"Good work, girls!" Katie exclaimed as she came out from her hiding place in the tree. "I think Dusty and James will be very happy together."

Shimmer scampered along a tree branch, purring loudly to show that he agreed, and the girls laughed.

"Fairy magic is wonderful!" Rachel said with a smile. She watched as Shimmer sniffed at a beetle on a nearby leaf and gave a tiny, fairy-sized sneeze.

Just then, Kirsty heard a rustling sound from a little higher up in the tree. She looked up to see a goblin— and then another— and then another! She gasped. There was a whole chain of grinning goblins hanging down from one branch of the tree! The lowest goblin was dangling just above the branch where Shimmer was perched. He was reaching out to grab the magic kitten!

"No, you don't!" cried Kirsty,
scooping up Shimmer, just in time.

"Give it here!" the goblin growled,
lunging after the kitten.

Shimmer meowed in alarm as the goblin's fingers came within a whisker of him. But the goblin had reached out too far, and the other goblins couldn't hold on to him. They all tumbled to the ground, landing in a big green pile of tangled arms and legs!

"Ouch! You're squishing me!" grumbled one goblin.

"Get off!" groaned another.

Katie grinned at the girls. "Come on! Let's go while we have the chance," she said.

Kirsty held out her hands and let Shimmer run through the air to Katie as they all walked away from the pile of grumpy goblins. "I don't think Jack Frost will be pleased when they come back empty-handed," Kirsty said, glancing back over her shoulder.

The goblins were still bickering!

"No, Jack Frost won't be happy,"
Katie agreed. She suddenly shivered.
"He'll send them out again to look for
another pet." She cuddled her kitten
tightly at the thought of it. "Let's get
you safely back to Fairyland, Shimmer,"
she said in her sweet voice. "Good-bye
girls—and thank you
for everything."

Katie hugged the
girls in turn, and then
Shimmer nuzzled his
tiny nose against each
of their faces.

"Good-bye, little
Shimmer," Kirsty
said, giggling as his
fur tickled her nose.

"It's been nice to meet you."

"Tell the other Pet Fairies
that we'll keep looking
for the other lost
pets," Rachel
added, blowing
Katie and
Shimmer a kiss.

"We will," Katie
promised. "Good-
bye!" She tucked
Shimmer carefully
under one arm,
then waved her
wand. A shower of
amber-colored lights
twinkled around Katie
and Shimmer, and then
they were gone.

Rachel and Kirsty smiled at each other and headed home. After all the excitement, they both felt hungry. "I'm so happy we found a nice home for Dusty," Rachel said with a smile. "Everything worked out perfectly. It couldn't have gone better!"

Kirsty slipped her arm through Rachel's as they walked out the park gate.

"I can't wait to find another one of the lost fairy pets," she said excitedly. "It looks like another fairy adventure isn't far away!"

Now it's time for Kirsty and
Rachel to help . . .

BELLA the BUNNY FAIRY.

Read on for a sneak peek . . .

EASTER BUNNY

"Isn't it a perfect day for a party?" Kirsty Tate said, looking up at the sapphire-blue sky.

Her best friend, Rachel Walker, nodded and handed Kirsty a chocolate egg. Rachel was staying with Kirsty for spring break, and the girls were busy hiding eggs. They were getting ready for

Jane, Mr. and Mrs. Dillon's five-year-old daughter. The Dillons lived down the street from Kirsty.

"There are some great hiding places here," Rachel said. She gazed around the beautiful yard full of green grass and colorful flower beds. Then she knelt down and hid the egg under a shrub. "Jane and her friends will love the Easter egg hunt!"

"It'll be fun," Kirsty agreed, hiding an egg behind the birdbath.

"How many children are invited to the party?" Rachel asked.

"Eleven!" Kirsty replied, her eyes twinkling. "Mr. and Mrs. Dillon are so glad that we're helping! They've been friends with my mom and dad for a long time, and Jane is really sweet." Then she lowered her voice. "Do you think we'll find another of the missing fairy pets today, Rachel?"

"I hope so," Rachel whispered back.

More Titles to Read
Collect them all!

THE RAINBOW FAIRIES

THE PET FAIRIES

SPECIAL EDITIONS

BEHIND THE MAGIC

DAISY MEADOWS is a pseudonym for the four writers of the internationally best-selling *Rainbow Magic* series: Narinder Dhami, Sue Bentley, Linda Chapman, and Sue Mongredien. *Rainbow Magic* is the No.1 best-selling series for children ages 5 and up, with over 40 million copies sold worldwide!

GEORGIE RIPPER was born in London and is a children's book illustrator known for her work on the *Rainbow Magic* series of fairy books. She won the Macmillan Prize for Picture Book Illustration in 2000 with *My Best Friend, Bob* and *Little Brown Bushrat*, which she wrote and illustrated.